Rr

Qq

Zz

Aa

Uu

Oo

M Is for MUSIC

M Is for

KATHLEEN KRULL

MUSIC

Illustrated by

STACY INNERST

Harcourt, Inc.

Orlando ∗ Austin ∗ New York ∗ San Diego ∗ Toronto ∗ London

www.HarcourtBooks.com

Library of Congress Cataloging-in-Publication Data
Krull, Kathleen.
M is for music/Kathleen Krull; illustrated by Stacy Innerst.
p. cm.
Summary: An alphabet book introducing musical terms, from allegro to zarzuela.
1. Music—Dictionaries, Juvenile.   2. Music—Miscellanea—Juvenile literature.
[1. Music.   2. Alphabet.]   I. Innerst, Stacy, ill.   II. Title.
ML3928.K78   2003
780'.3—dc21   2002013037
ISBN 0-15-201438-1

C E G H F D

Manufactured in China

For all those who make music
—K. K.

For Lynne
and our background music,
Stuart, Olivia, and Jake
—S. I.

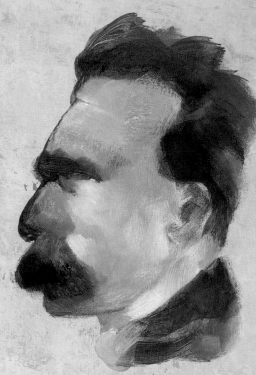

"Without music, life would
be a mistake."

—Friedrich Nietzsche

"Music is your own experience,
your own thoughts, your wisdom."

—Charlie Parker

"Hear the music of voices, the song of the bird, the mighty strains of an orchestra, as if you would be stricken deaf tomorrow."

—Helen Keller

"Without music to decorate it, time is just a bunch of boring production deadlines and dates by which bills must be paid."

—Frank Zappa

Aa is for anthem and accordion.

a cappella

aria

Louis Armstrong

B b is for Beatles.

bongo

BRAHMS

BACH

beat

band

bass

banjo

ballad

Beethoven

BROADWAY

bluegrass

bassoon

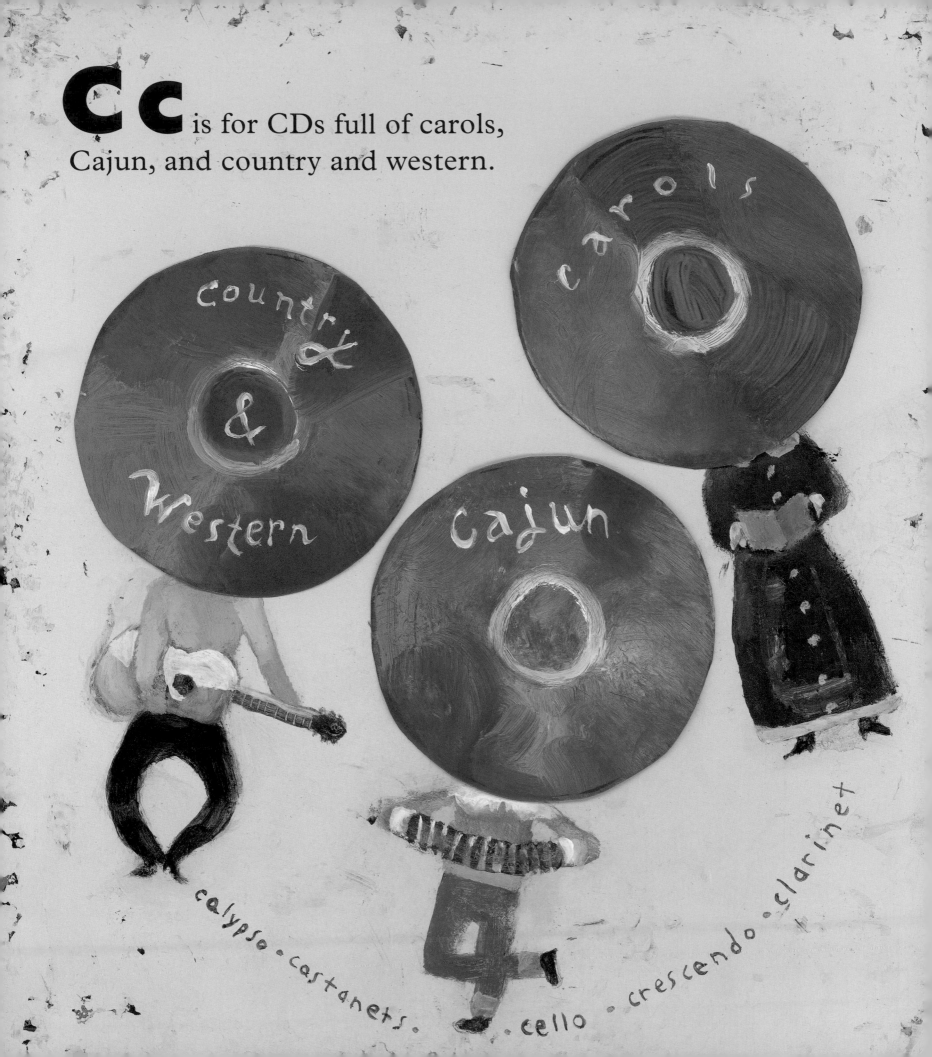

Cc

is for CDs full of carols,
Cajun, and country and western.

country & western

carols

Cajun

calypso • castanets • cello • crescendo • clarinet

do re mi

duet

disco

dulcimer

Dd is for dancing and drumming all around your house.

Ee is for Elvis, energy, and encore.

E·A·R

electric guitar

elevator music

echo

falsetto • French horn

flute

fa la la la la

"This land is your land"

flamenco

Ff
is for finger-snapping
folk song.

Gg is for guitar.

GROOVE

Gilbert & Sullivan

Hh is for Hildegard and harp.

harmony   hymn   harmonica   humming   Handel

I i is for interesting instrument.

Jug band Jive

Jitterbug

J j is for jazz.

Jim session

jig   jukebox

Kk **is for klezmer.**

Ll is for LOUD!

"When in doubt,
sing loud."
—Robert Merrill,
American singer

M m is for music,
music teachers (where would we be without them?),
mistakes (everyone makes them),
and Mozart (makes you smarter).

maraca

MOTOWN

Nn is for *The Nutcracker.*

Pp
is for piano and practice,
practice, practice.

percussion . pitch . prodigy

performance

Prokofiev

P
O
L
K
A

piccolo

Qq is for quartet and quintet.

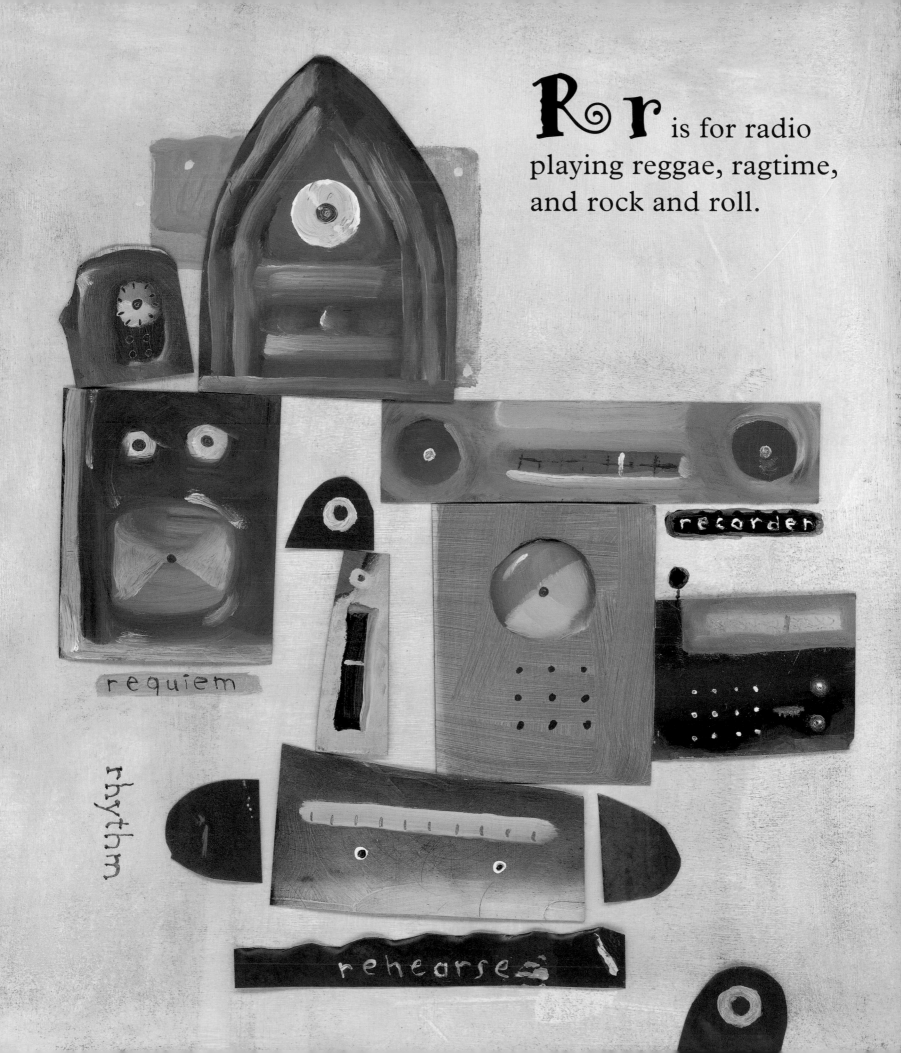

R r is for radio
playing reggae, ragtime,
and rock and roll.

recorder

requiem

rhythm

rehearse

Saxophone

ROOMS

Cafe

Sitar

Soprano

Ss is for street musician singing
show tunes, spirituals, and serenades.

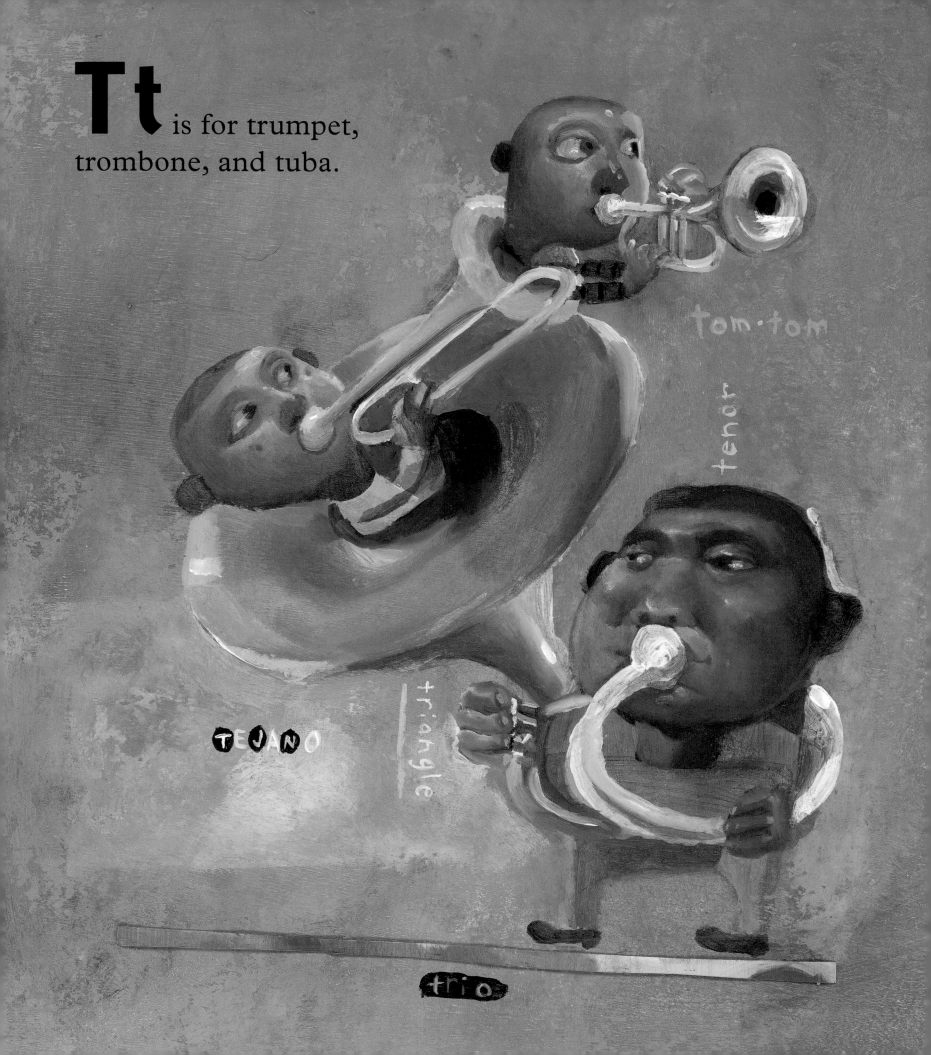

Tt is for trumpet, trombone, and tuba.

U u is for ukuleles in unison.

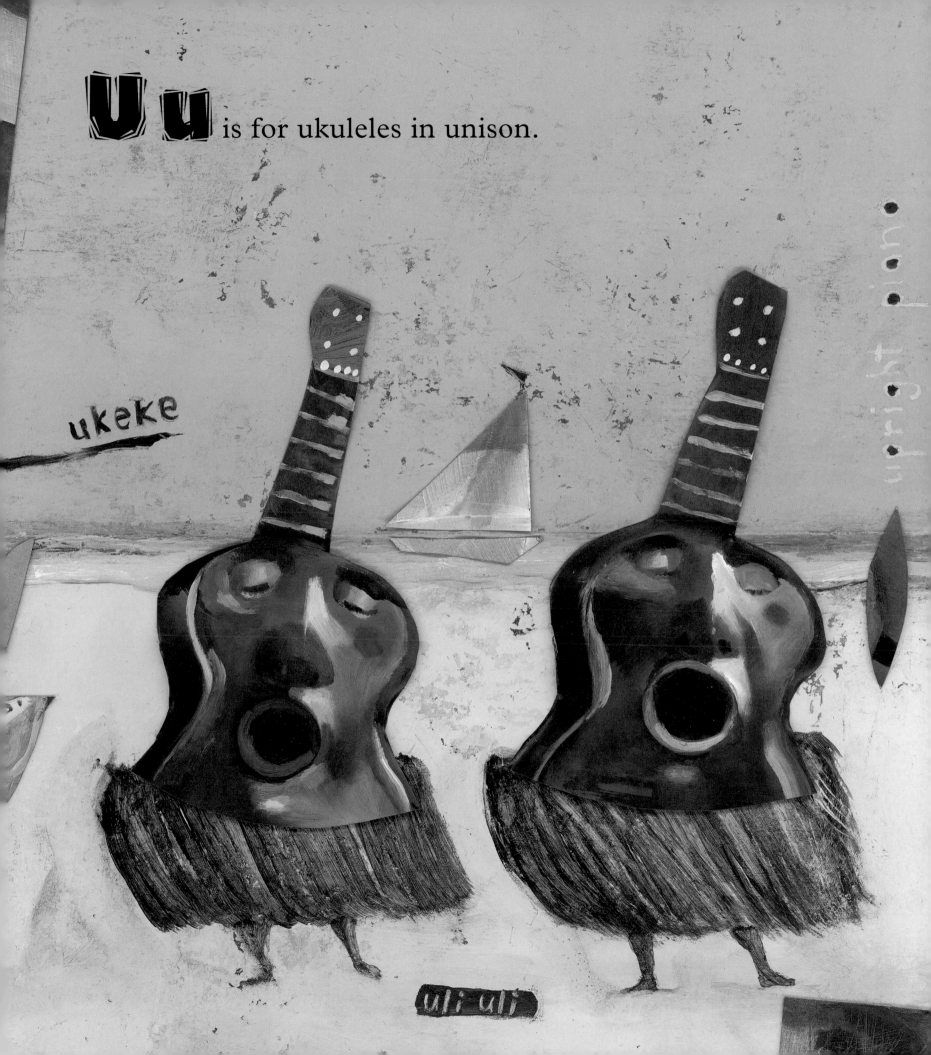

ukeke

upright piano

uli uli

Vv is for voice and vibration.

Vocals

Volume

Viola

Violin

- VIRTUOSO -

woodwinds

waltz

world
music

washboard

W w is for whistling.

X x is for experimental music on a xylophone.

Yy is for yodeling "Yankee Doodle."

Zz is for zydeco, zither, and all forms of zippy music!

zapateado

zarzuela

Musical Notes from A to Z

Aa An **anthem** is a short vocal work expressing patriotic or religious feelings. Almost every country has an official anthem that conveys national pride. "The Star-Spangled Banner" is the national anthem of the United States. It's not often played on the accordion, but it could be! The **accordion,** invented in 1822 but related to an ancient Chinese instrument, has a boxy shape, a piano-like keyboard, and a joyous sound.

Bb In the 1960s, a phenomenon known as Beatlemania centered on the **Beatles,** a British rock-and-roll group. The most popular band in history had a traditional rock group formation: lead guitar (George Harrison), bass guitar and vocals (Paul McCartney), rhythm guitar and vocals (John Lennon), and drums (Ringo Starr). Many former Beatlemaniacs, now parents, raise their children on Beatles music.

Cc Compact discs, or **CDs,** are an evolution in technology that began with the phonograph record; the phonograph was invented by American Thomas Edison in 1877. The first song ever played on one was "Mary Had a Little Lamb." CDs capture every kind of music, including **carols** (seasonal religious songs usually associated with Christmas), **Cajun** (a Louisiana blend of African and European influences—impossible not to dance to), and **country and western** (songs about ordinary working people; superstars include Jimmie Rodgers, Dolly Parton, Tammy Wynette, and Johnny Cash).

D d   Music and rhythmic bodily movement have always gone together. **Dancing** can take place on a stage, in a ballroom, or at a rock concert, but it's especially fun at home. Find a special place somewhere in your house to dance to your favorite music. For a dancing beat, nothing beats **drums.** Throughout history, drums have been important for performing rituals, sending messages, whipping up energy, getting people to *move.* Every culture in the world (notably American Indian and African) takes advantage of drum power.

E e   **Elvis** Presley, the "King of Rock and Roll" (1935–1977), is possibly the most popular musician of all time. With his combination of rhythm and blues and country and western, he dominated rock music until the arrival of the Beatles. Elvis's music is full of **energy,** a sensation that music can give. Something about music just makes us react—legs start jumping, hands start twitching. Even the way humans are "wired"—our pulse, a baby's sense of its mother's heartbeat, our walking and breathing—is instinctively rhythmic. To shout **encore** means "More, more, more!"

F f   Snapping our **fingers** helps us keep a beat and is one of many physical reactions we have to music. **Folk songs** like "Michael, Row the Boat Ashore" and "On Top of Old Smoky" are popular tunes that originated among ordinary people. Not written down, often national or regional in character, they're passed orally from one generation to the next. Songs by American Woody Guthrie (like "This Land Is Your Land") have been passed around so much that they are considered honorary folk songs.

G g   The **guitar** typically has six strings, a long neck, and a curvy middle. It showed up in Spain in the early sixteenth century and became wildly popular. Today it is essential to popular and folk music throughout the United States and Europe and is second only to the piano in its popularity with amateur musicians. The electric guitar, invented in the 1940s, is synonymous with rock music.

H h

Hildegard of Bingen (1098–1179), a German nun, is the first woman composer we know by name. Now, more than eight hundred years later, her music is very popular. Until the last century or two, many cultures discouraged or even forbade women from pursuing musical activities, making Hildegard's accomplishments amazing for her time. The **harp** is found in almost every country in the world. The earliest musical instrument to have survived until modern times is a harp from what is now Iraq—it dates back to 2600 B.C.

I i

Instruments are objects we use to make music. Early people used rocks, sticks, shells, seeds, and animal bones. Musical instruments have since evolved into the most sophisticated of inventions that can produce virtually any sound. In a one-man band, one person plays all the instruments, often at the same time!

J j

Jazz originated with African Americans in early twentieth-century New Orleans. Early jazz greats include Jelly Roll Morton, Louis Armstrong, Duke Ellington, and Charlie Parker. A rule-breaking, all new sound at the time, it is now considered the United States's outstanding contribution to musical history.

K k

Klezmer, popular in the United States today, is rooted in traditional Jewish party music from Eastern Europe. Klezmer bands feature instruments such as clarinets, accordions, violins, and, occasionally, voices.

L l

Doesn't your favorite music sound better when it's **loud**? Singing, loud or soft, is one of the most creative ways to express yourself. It's good for every part of your body, especially your lungs. In fact, doctors recommend singing as a way to get over bronchitis—it helps keep the lungs clear. Singing in front of people might seem scary, but doing it loudly can increase your confidence.

Mm   **Music** is the art of arranging sound and rhythm to give a desired effect. The earliest music came from primitive cave dwellers experimenting with tricks their voices could do. Since then **music teachers** have heroically guided us past **mistakes** we make while we try to perfect our art. Many people consider the perfect, mistake-free composer to be Wolfgang Amadeus **Mozart** (1756–1791), the Austrian genius who mastered the piano by age four and composed by age five. In recent years scientists have said that listening to Mozart's music seems to enhance memory and learning skills. Music in general appears to make you smarter: Experiments have shown that young children who participate regularly in musical activities have more highly developed skills in mathematics and spatial relationships than their nonmusical peers.

Nn   ***The Nutcracker*** is a ballet by Russian composer Peter Ilich Tchaikovsky, based on a fairy tale by E. T. A. Hoffmann. A girl named Clara receives a mysterious nutcracker, which comes alive, battles the Mouse King, and turns into a handsome prince. Popular at Christmastime, *The Nutcracker* has introduced more children to classical music than any other composition in history.

Oo   An **orchestra** is the largest formal group of musicians. Music (notably classical music) has been written specifically for orchestras for four centuries, and much of that music is still performed today. Orchestras vary in size, but generally have four main instrument sections: strings, woodwinds, brass, and percussion. The players sit in a semicircle in front of the conductor. **"Old MacDonald Had a Farm"** is an old English-American folk song that can be continued for as long as you can think of farm animals to sing about.

Pp   Invented in 1709, the **piano** was the first instrument in the keyboard family that could be played loudly or softly by using finger pressure. Before the invention of radio and TV, families often gathered around the piano for sing-alongs. The piano remains the most popular instrument of amateur musicians. **"Practice, practice, practice"** is the motto of every serious musician.

Qq A **quartet** (a musical group of four) can be made up of any instruments, but in classical music typically consists of two violins, a viola, and a cello. A **quintet** adds another viola or cello; a piano quintet is not five pianos but rather one piano plus a string quartet.

Rr The **radio,** a great popularizer of all types of music, is a relatively recent invention. Its first broadcasts in the United States were made in 1906. You can turn on your radio and hear **reggae** (a style that originated in Jamaica in the mid-1960s); **ragtime** (an early type of jazz with a "ragged" rhythm; American Scott Joplin is its most famous composer); and especially **rock and roll** (a uniquely popular and vibrant blend of jazz, gospel, country, rhythm and blues, and soul, originating in the 1950s).

Ss **Street musicians** entertain us in the most unexpected outdoor locations with almost any kind of music, including **show tunes** (from musicals often performed in the famed theater district on Broadway, a street in New York City); **spirituals** (deeply emotional, religious songs that originated with African Americans in the South); and **serenades** (traditionally, songs played at night under the window of a loved one).

Tt The slender **trumpet,** sliding **trombone,** and bulky **tuba** are three of the principal brass instruments. They really are made of brass, but have evolved from instruments made from such natural materials as animal horns, conch shells, and hollow branches. Playing them requires tremendous lip control and can make musicians turn purple from the hard work.

Uu The **ukulele** is a tiny guitar with four strings that originated in Portugal and became most popular in the South Pacific islands. **Unison** means "all together now."

V v   The versatile **voice** is the human means of producing sound, which happens when our vocal cords vibrate. Voices can range from the deep bass to tenor to alto to the very highest soprano. **Vibrations** (or vibes) are what all music is made of: the side-to-side motion of vibrations creates sound.

W w   **Whistles** were some of the earliest instruments. Prehistoric people made whistles from reindeer toe bones as far back as 40,000 B.C. Humans imitate the ancient sound by puckering their lips to do their own **whistling.**

X x   Breaking the rules is the job of e**x**perimental music; the American composer John Cage (1912–1992) is one of experimental music's biggest rule breakers. The **xylophone** developed from primitive people's signaling each other by banging two slabs of wood together.

Y y   **Yodeling,** first developed in Austria, is a type of singing that alternates between natural voice and falsetto. **"Yankee Doodle,"** America's unofficial national anthem, was popularized during the Revolutionary War. It would be difficult to yodel "Yankee Doodle," but why don't you try it?

Z z   **Zydeco** is a variation of Cajun music from Louisiana. The **zither** is a sound box across which strings are stretched and plucked with the fingers. The simplest one is found in Africa and Southeast Asia—the ground zither, which consists of strings stretched across a small hole in the ground.

The illustrations in this book were done in oils and
acrylics on a surface of gessoed board and tin.
The display type was set in Remedy and Victoria Casual.
The text type was set in Plantin.
Color separations by Bright Arts Ltd., Hong Kong
Manufactured by South China Printing Company, Ltd., China
This book was printed on totally chlorine-free Enso Stora Matte paper.
Production supervision by Sandra Grebenar and Pascha Gerlinger
Designed by Ivan Holmes